Disney

A Storybook Treasury

101 Dalmatians is based on the original book The Hundred and One Dalmatians by Dodie Smith, published by The Viking Press.

For information address Disney Press, 114 Fifth Avenue, New York, New York 10011-5690.
Printed in China
10 9 8 7 6 5 4 3 2 1
ISBN 1-4231-0561-3
Visit www.disneybooks.com

Disney

A Storybook Treasury

DISNEY
PRESS

New York

Contents

Walt Disney's

Bambi

One beautiful spring morning a little rabbit named Thumper woke Friend Owl with some wonderful news. A baby deer had been born deep in the woods. "It's happened!" cried the little rabbit. "A new prince is born!"

"What's his name?" asked the animals.

"Why, his name is Bambi," his mother replied.

Soon Bambi met all the other wonderful animals in the forest. First Mrs. Quail and her

babies stopped to say hello. Then Mrs. Opossum and her family, who liked to hang upside down, smiled at Bambi. Next, a mole poked his head out from underground to wish Bambi a good day. Even a flock of little bluebirds flew down to greet the young prince.

Bambi made friends with Thumper and a shy little

skunk called Flower. They laughed and played

together every

day. Soon, at

the pond in the

meadow, Bambi

made another

friend — a

playful girl

fawn named

Faline.

Summer and fall passed happily for Bambi. And when the cold winter came, Thumper taught Bambi how to spin and slide on the frozen pond. Bambi had never done anything like this before. "C'mon, it's all right," Thumper told him, gliding across the ice. "The water's stiff!"

Finally winter was over and the spring brought many changes. Bambi had grown into a handsome young buck.

His friends Thumper and Flower had grown up, too. Friend Owl couldn't get over them. He was sure that any moment now they would all meet somebody and become… twitterpated. That meant they would fall in love.

The three friends laughed at the wise old owl and agreed to spend all their time together — until Flower met a lovely girl skunk and got twitterpated. Bambi knew he would miss Flower. But at least he and Thumper could still spend time together. Then

Thumper fell in love, too!

Next it was Bambi's turn. Soon he met a beautiful

doe in the meadow. It was his old friend Faline!

Bambi suddenly felt dizzy and light as a feather! He

was twitterpated, too! Bambi and Faline frolicked together just as they had done in the meadow when they were young.

But Bambi wasn't the only buck who liked Faline. A stag named Ronno soon pushed his way between them, challenging Bambi to a fierce fight. Bambi charged Ronno with all his might, and the two bucks butted heads again and again. Finally, Bambi won the

fight. And from that day on, he and Faline were always together.

One fall morning Bambi smelled something strange — smoke. Just then a majestic stag appeared.

It was Bambi's father, the Great Prince. "The forest is on fire!" he cried. "Hurry! We must warn the other animals to run to the river island."

Bambi and the Prince warned all the forest

animals. Then they crossed the river, where they

found Faline waiting for them. Bambi and his friends

watched as fire destroyed their forest homes and

everything around them.

After the fire was out, the old stag turned to

Bambi. "I must leave you now," he said. "You will

take my place as Prince of the Forest." Bambi knew

this was a great responsibility, but he was ready to

accept it.

When the last bit of smoke was gone, the animals

bravely rebuilt their homes.

Fall once again turned into winter and winter into

spring. The forest
was lush and green
and smelled of
blooming flowers.

Soon Thumper
and his little
bunnies were
waking Friend Owl

once again. Faline had given birth to twin fawns. All
the animals proudly came to celebrate.

But no one was prouder than Bambi, the new
Prince of the Forest. He stood overlooking the

thicket, smiling down on his family, his heart filled with love. Soon, Bambi would teach them the lessons of the forest that he himself had learned so long ago.

Walt Disney's Peter Pan

Long ago, in the city of London, there lived a family named Darling. Wendy, John, and Michael Darling would sit in the nursery telling stories about a far-off place called Never Land where the daring Peter Pan and the pixie Tinker Bell lived.

And no one in Never Land ever grew old.

Peter Pan and Tinker Bell came to the Darling's nursery window one night to get Peter's shadow. It wasn't Peter's first visit to the Darling house.

He had come there many times to listen to Wendy's stories. Peter was upset when Wendy explained that this was to be her last night in the nursery.

"But that means no more stories," cried Peter, "unless I take you all back to Never Land with me."

"That would be wonderful," the children shouted. Everyone but Tinker Bell agreed.

"But how will we get there?" Wendy asked.

"All you've got to do is fly," Peter replied.

And, with a sprinkle of pixie dust from Tinker Bell, they soared through the skies of London and all the way to Peter's Never Land home.

Down below they saw waterfalls and the Mermaid Lagoon. There was a pirate ship, a forest, and even an Indian camp.

The pirate ship belonged to Captain Hook. The captain had two enemies in Never Land — Peter Pan

and a hungry crocodile. One day, in a fight with Peter,

the crocodile had gotten a taste of Hook's hand and

had followed him around ever since, hoping for more.

Hook blamed Peter Pan.

When the friends got to Never Land, Peter took

Wendy, Michael, and John into the forest to meet the Lost Boys.

Then he and Wendy went to visit the Mermaid Lagoon. There Peter spied the Indian Chief's daughter, Tiger Lily, tied up in Captain Hook's boat. They heard Hook ask Tiger Lily to reveal Peter's

hiding place. But the Indian princess wouldn't tell him anything.

"I have to save Tiger Lily!" Peter cried. He and Wendy followed Captain Hook to Skull Rock. Peter challenged the pirate to a duel. But Peter was too fast and too smart for Hook. With one quick lunge, Hook landed in the water next to the hungry crocodile — his greatest fear.

Peter rescued
Tiger Lily and
brought her back
to the Indian
camp.

Captain Hook
got away from the
crocodile and
swore revenge

against Peter Pan. He kidnapped Tinker Bell and

tricked her into telling him where Peter lived.

Then the pirates went to Peter's hideout and

captured Wendy, John, Michael, and the Lost Boys.

Knowing that Peter would never be able to resist a beautifully wrapped package, the pirates left a present in the tree house for him. As soon as he opened it, BOOM, it would explode! And that would be the end of Peter Pan.

Tinker Bell knew what Hook had planned. She had to warn Peter before it was too late! She made her escape carefully and flew back to the hideout.

"Peter Pan will save us," Wendy insisted as she was

about to walk the plank.

But the evil captain just laughed at her. "Pan will

never save you now!" he cried with glee.

Captain Hook did not realize that Tinker Bell was

already on her way to get Peter.

Peter and Tinker Bell returned in a flash. "Hook, this time you've gone too far!" Peter shouted as he challenged him to one last duel.

Wendy, Michael, John, and the Lost Boys watched in awe as Peter fought so bravely to save them. At last Hook and the pirates ended up in the water. They swam as fast as they could, with the always-hungry crocodile close behind.

"Thank you so much for saving us," said Wendy. "And now I think it's time for us to go back home."

Before they could say "Captain Hook," Peter set sail in Hook's very own ship through the skies of Never Land.

They were soon back in London safe and sound.

Peter and Tinker Bell said their good-byes, and the Darlings promised never to forget the wonderful times they had. As the years went by, they would remember everything — Peter, Tinker Bell, the pirates, Tiger Lily, and the Lost Boys — just as if it had all happened yesterday.

Pongo, Perdita, and their fifteen puppies lived in a cozy little house in London. The house belonged to their humans, Roger and Anita. They were perfectly happy until they met Cruella De Vil — Anita's old schoolmate who simply loved spotted puppies.

She wanted to buy them all and make them into spotted fur coats!

Roger put his foot down. "These puppies are not for sale and that's final!"

Cruella was furious but she refused to give up.

One night Cruella's two nasty henchmen, Horace

and Jasper, kidnapped the puppies! Then they drove

out to Cruella's old country estate and waited to hear from their boss.

When the puppies got there, they saw lots and lots of other Dalmatian puppies who had also been snatched by Horace and Jasper.

Back at home, Pongo and Perdita could not believe what had happened.

Perdita knew  at once that Cruella was behind her missing puppies.

"She has stolen them," sobbed Perdita. "Oh, Pongo, do you think we'll ever find them?"

Pongo knew that the Twilight Bark was their only hope. He would bark his message to the dogs in London. They would pick it up and pass it along to the dogs in the country. And maybe someone would find the puppies.

That night the Twilight Bark reached a quiet farm where an old English sheepdog known as Colonel lay sleeping peacefully.

"Alert, alert!" shouted Sergeant Tibs, a cat who lived on the farm. "Vital message coming in from London."

The Colonel listened closely. "Fifteen puppies have been stolen!" he cried.

Sergeant Tibs remembered hearing barking at the old De Vil place. They headed straight for the gloomy mansion.

The Colonel helped Tibs look through the window. Sure enough, there were the fifteen puppies — plus their eighty-four new friends!

Tibs and the Colonel overheard Cruella, Jasper, and Horace talking. When they heard Cruella's plans to make coats out of the puppies, they knew there was no time to waste. The Colonel ran off to get word to Pongo and Perdita while Tibs helped the puppies escape!

As soon as Horace and Jasper realized what was

happening, they tried to stop the puppies. But it was too late. Pongo and Perdita arrived and fought off the foolish thugs as the puppies hurried to safety.

Once all the dogs were out of the house, they

thanked the Colonel and Tibs and went on their way.

A black Labrador retriever arranged for them to ride

to London in the back of a moving van that was being

repaired. The dogs waited in a blacksmith's shop.

Suddenly Cruella's big car drove up the street. She

had followed their tracks and was parked and waiting.

But Pongo had a clever idea. There were ashes in

the fireplace. If they all rolled in them, they would be disguised in black soot. Then they could get aboard

the van without Cruella realizing it was them! And that's just what they did.

It worked perfectly until a glob of snow dripped onto a puppy and washed off a patch of soot. From her car, Cruella could see it was a Dalmatian puppy.

"They're escaping!" she cried as the van took off.

The chase was on until Cruella tried to pass the van on the road. She ended up crashing through a barricade and driving right into a huge pile of snow. Cruella's beautiful car was a wreck! And that wasn't all. She had lost the puppies! Cruella threw a tantrum.

Pongo and Perdita and 99 puppies arrived home

safely, much to

Roger and Anita's

delight. Roger pulled

out a handkerchief

and wiped Pongo's

face clean.

"What will we

do with all these

puppies?" Anita

asked.

"We'll keep them," Roger answered. He sat down at the piano and composed a song right on the spot. "We'll buy a big place in the country, and we'll have a plantation," he sang. "A Dalmatian plantation!"

And that's exactly what they did.

Disney's THE RETURN OF JAFAR

Iago to the Rescue

All was well in Agrabah. The evil sorcerer Jafar was defeated and imprisoned in his lamp. Aladdin and Abu had a new home at the palace with Princess Jasmine and the Sultan. And Genie was back from his trip around the world.

"I got souvenirs for everybody!" he exclaimed.

And, to top it all off, the Sultan had made Aladdin his Royal Vizier — his most trusted

adviser. Imagine the Sultan's surprise at Aladdin's first official piece of advice: to allow Jafar's old sidekick, Iago the parrot, to stay at the palace. Now that Iago was out from under Jafar's spell, Aladdin thought he could be trusted.

The Sultan was skeptical, but he agreed — as long as Aladdin kept an eye on Iago.

Meanwhile, out in the desert, a thief named Abis Mal had found Jafar's lamp — and rubbed it. Jafar was back!

"You will help me get revenge on a certain street rat by the name of Aladdin!" Jafar commanded Abis Mal. The Rules of the Genie prevented Jafar from harming Aladdin himself. He promised Abis Mal a huge reward in exchange for his help.

Next, Jafar tracked down Iago. "I'm arranging a little... *surprise* for Aladdin, and your job is to lead him to the party," Jafar said to Iago.

Iago tried to resist. After all, he and Aladdin were just getting to be friends. But Jafar was more powerful than ever.

Iago had no choice. He went to Aladdin and
suggested that Aladdin take the Sultan for a scenic
ride on the Magic Carpet. "And I...I can take you
to the perfect spot,"
the parrot added.

Aladdin agreed.
He had no idea that
Jafar would be
there, invisible,
controlling Iago, and leading Aladdin into a trap. The
evil sorcerer was watching Aladdin's every move.

Away they flew — Aladdin, the Sultan, and Iago — on the Magic Carpet. The Sultan was having the time of his life.

"Come on, my boy," he said to Aladdin. "Show me what this thing can really do!"

Only Iago knew about the danger that awaited them at their destination.

Back at the palace, Jafar made sure that Genie and Abu were out of the way. "I can't have any genies mucking about, ruining my plans," Jafar said evilly. He overpowered Genie, encasing him in a crystal sphere, and shackled Abu.

Then Jafar transformed himself into a small army of masked riders on winged stallions. Together, the riders and Abis Mal flew off and kidnapped the Sultan as he, Aladdin,  and Iago lounged near the top of a giant waterfall.

Aladdin tried to rescue the Sultan, but Jafar's magic was too strong. Aladdin fell into the water and was swept away by the raging river. Then, just before Aladdin was thrown against some jagged rocks, Jafar summoned his magic… and spared his life!

"It is not yet time for the boy to meet his end," Jafar said to Abis Mal.

As Aladdin made his way home on foot, Jafar flew ahead to the palace to set the next phase of his plan in motion. In a palace dungeon, he held the Sultan, Jasmine, Genie, Abu, and the Magic Carpet captive. Then, disguised as Jasmine, he told the palace guards that the Sultan was dead, and that Aladdin was guilty of the crime!

Aladdin finally reached the palace, exhausted and worried about the Sultan. The guards immediately arrested him. At dawn, they prepared to

execute Aladdin for the murder of the Sultan.

Meanwhile, inside the palace dungeon, Iago strained to lift the crystal sphere that held Genie. Iago wanted to regain Aladdin's trust. If he could just get the crystal high enough…

Crash! Iago dropped the sphere, shattering it. In a flash, Genie flew out the window and scooped up Aladdin before the executioner's blade fell.

Genie freed the Sultan, Jasmine, and the others. Now they just had to stop Jafar.

"You destroy Jafar's lamp, you destroy Jafar," Genie advised them.

Both Aladdin and Jasmine went after the lamp.

But Jafar was onto them. And in his most powerful form as the evil genie, Jafar was a force to be reckoned with.

In his fury, Jafar ripped holes in the earth. Soon the palace grounds became a bubbling pool of hot lava. Aladdin jumped on the Magic Carpet and struggled to stay out of the fiery lava while chasing after the lamp. But mighty Jafar managed to keep it just out of Aladdin's reach.

Then, just when it looked as if Jafar had won, Iago swooped down and snatched the lamp.

"Traitor!" Jafar screamed, striking Iago with a fireball. The bird and the lamp landed on a ledge. With his last ounce of strength, Iago kicked the lamp into the fiery lava below.

"Noooooo!" screamed Jafar, as his lamp melted away and he began to spin faster and faster... until he disappeared forever!

It was official: Iago had definitely regained Aladdin's trust. And so the bird lived happily ever after, wallowing in luxury as Aladdin's "palace pal."